Lightning's Limit

(A Cypher Theorem Story)

By:

Mark Brandon Powell

Mark Brandon Powell

Contents

1

The sun rises with a faint orange glow penetrating through the dome of Pharis. Vargas was used to getting up this early but it's usually just to make it to class on time. It felt strange going to school on an off day. He didn't have to follow dress code but he did have to have some school work ready. It was tournament day and nothing could be more exciting.

Pedaling his bike the whole way there was tiring, and mostly for training because he always trained but partly because it is an older model bicycle who's magnetic drive system, or magdrive, was broken. He hadn't fixed it yet because his finances were tight and with it being good for his physical conditioning he didn't want to save the extra money just yet to get it fixed. Everyone at school liked to pass judgment upon the poor boy from the edge of the dome. He could have some of the frills of life if he wanted them but he didn't.

Vargas should have slept like a stone the night before, after a hard day of school, practice, and apprenticeship but didn't. He has been wound up for some time now, with the tournament getting so close, he thinks when was the last time he had a good night's rest. Had it been a week, month, year... Vargas' mind wandered... how long had it really been? He has been on a streak of luck, starting with gaining an apprenticeship with *the* Seleaf Mativ, a highly accomplished Sage, and that was two years ago.

Also since the council just approved to hold the Magical Martial Arts tournaments this school year, his whole life had been turned into work, apprenticeship, work in between semesters and school, practice, apprenticeship, work during. But even before that, it hadn't been easy with his dad working three jobs just to scrape by with the high cost of living in Pharis over the last 9 years.

He missed his mother every day since she was murdered. With his dad having to picking up the slack in the income, it was almost like he lost both his parents that day. But today he wasn't going to think about any of that and was going to make this day be a great day all around. It was the first official MMA tournament, and his father promised to give him a ride home from the arena, and he knew he would find a time and place to use everything Master Sel taught him.

'*Only in life threatening situations.*' Master Sel's caveat kept resonating in Vargas' head over and over about a rune symbol he had shown him. He also said something about delorium metal with its half life of about 4 seconds. He remembered that him saying this rune worked best on that metal. '*It's forged in a special rune chamber that alters time and master time elementals cast powerful and focused spells to make that 4 second half life into something akin to regular steel but molecularly stronger than a diamond. It is extremely time consuming, ironically enough, to forge with...*'

Vargas remembered most of speech just not exactly as it was spoken. He was just waiting for his '*life threatening situation*' to come up. He may not have perfectly listened or remembered everything Master Sel said but he knew he was serious from the tone given. All he had to do was inscribe the rune on the ground, because only the planet is strong enough to support the pressure of magical power this rune can exert, other than delorium. All he needs now is the right opening and once drawn he was going to blow the other teams away.

He was the first one to arrive at the school, other than Coach Hillborn, he got off his bike and folded it up into his bag and walked toward the bus.

"You're early as usual Mitchell."

"I am, how are you doing coach?"

"Doing good, and I hope no one gets hurt today at the tournament."

"What about us winning it?"

"Mitchell, throw your bag in the storage let's talk about that."

"Oh! Do want to talk strategy? How about the Hillborn hand block? Or maybe the Pharis fetal position? Or if things get dicey we can run that trick play where we all get in Julie's mirage field and-"

"Mitchell, you know that bothers me as much as it bothers you. Just like I told you two weeks ago, we have to keep the rich kids safe. Rich kids have rich parents and rich parents pay off school admins to put rich kids as team captains. If a team captain gets hurt, my boss gets hurt, right where it counts."

"I know, right in the wallet."

"That's right. Look, I know you can do more and I'm actually looking forward to seeing it, but as long as I have verbal orders, it's going to be drills, drills, drills to keep them occupied during practice and it will all be defense, defense, defense, to try to keep them somewhat safe in a real match."

"I know coach, and thanks for sharing that with me. I still haven't told that to anyone. I was just giving you a hard time since no one was here yet. Speaking of which, I was wondering if I could get your help on some history. I was supposed to have it finished for class yesterday but Mr. Black said I could send it to him as long as I was on the schools network and before we leave today."

"Don't you have the check software the school provides?"

"No I don't."

Vargas would have loved to have signed up for the school's work check program but didn't have the extra credits each month to have his work validated like that through his HaLO. Everyone on Eden may be fitted with a Haptics Language and Optics bracelet at birth, but that didn't mean they were all born equal.

"Alright, what's the question?"

"I'm still a little unclear as to why people came here. I'm glad we did but why don't we try to go back to Earth?"

Coach Hillborn put on the best thinking face a coach can have when not looking at a play book and simply said, "From the way I understand it, we didn't have any magic there. They only had weapons, like guns and bombs. Some of those people would come up with a weapon that no one else had and then they would dominate without fear of retribution. That is of course until the other side copied or improved upon that weapon. Then it was flipped, and back and forth. Then one side finally made a weapon that was so big that it would not only kill far, and wide, but also over time."

"So it wasn't enough to just blow up whatever they were aiming at, they also had to make sure no one could use it?"

"Exactly. It was rarely used, until it was used frequently. It didn't take long after that to make the planet pretty inhospitable. As the old saying goes, peeing in your own bed and all."

Vargas was quickly jotting down notes during this impromptu session because the teachers are not usually so candid. He stops and looks up at Coach Hillborn and asks, "That was when Adam Augustus made the Ark, Aspiration, took everyone that wanted to go and flew off for here?"

"Exactly. It wasn't the only one, just the only Ark that we know survived."

"Thanks Coach. This should get me what I need. I'm going to go turn this in real quick."

Walking back out to the bus he sees all the girls are finally here. Amber walks over to him and says hello. She is the teams healer and is a shy girl whom doesn't have many friends. She's also the only one truly nice to him within the sea of the privileged he is in. She spends most of her time in the test lab learning new healing techniques or at volunteer hospitals using what she knows. He's just happy to have at least one friend in this place.

As they walk back to the bus talking about what's going to happen today, Julie appears beside them as they talk about their chances at winning the tournament today. Vargas looks over and can see that she doesn't realize that her spell has worn off. He decides to play a joke on her.

"So Amber, I just wanted to tell you something that you might be able to help with."

Amber looks over to Vargas and sees Julie between them, and answers Vargas without any surprise in her voice. "What might that be Vargas?"

"Well you see Julie confided in me the other day, and told me that she was in love with me."

Julie blurts out, "No I did not!", followed by her covering her mouth.

Vargas gets a big grin on his face as he says, "Well then you shouldn't be spying on people. You don't want people to hear a rumor about you falling in love with the poor kid."

Julie starts to turn four different shades of red in anger, "I swear Vargas if you tell anyone that I will have your head on a platter."

"Well you would have to catch me first." He says as he directs the flow of magic in his body down to his feet. Starting with just a spark of electricity to a full bolt of lightning that he arcs around behind Julie and rides to get behind her and whispers in her ear, "And you're not fast enough to catch me."

Julie turns to slap him in the face but she hits nothing but air. He is already back standing next to Amber.

Coach Hillborn yells out from the bus, "Julie Brawn please stop using your illusion magic outside of lessons to spy on people."

"But people get paid really good money to do that, I have to practice sometime." She retorts.

"Yes yes, you're going to be a big spy one day but not today. Load up on the bus so we can head out to Bastion."

Vargas heads toward the middle of the bus and takes a window seat and the bus slowly fills with the girls as they each have their chauffeurs take their luggage to the underside storage compartment of the bus. They all sit toward the front of the bus and begin gossiping about everything that had happen the week prior. Vargas rolls his eyes, and pulls up his overlay. He scrolls through his songs he has on his HaLO because he would rather listen to music than those girls chattering on the whole way there.

The ride through the dome was quick as they pull up toward the gates that leads out. The gates themselves are massive in size. There are three of them in total and each are as thick as the bus is long. As they approach each go through an opening process that unhinges and spins out of the way. Once though, waiting at the next door, the one behind spins closed, creating a seal before the next can open.

Trees cover the road on either side of the bus and Vargas is shocked to see as much technology as he does on the drive there. Digital advertisements attached to trees and rocks, that can only be seen when your overlay is active and full connectivity to the net. He had overhead a few boys talking about when they left the dome for vacations. They must have been talking about further out than what they are or it could all be hearsay.

Passing through the forest they come out to the open sky and a clear field and view of Bastion in the distance. The sun shining off the water and buildings through the ever thinning tree line. The Coliseum is clearly visible from the road and is the largest structure there. The closer they get the larger it becomes. It almost starts to almost intimidate Vargas.

Thoughts of doubt start running through his head, is he ready to do this, is he good enough, just because a sage taught you a few things who do you think you are to win something like this, and you're nothing but a poor kid from the dome you have no right to be here. Amber looks back and sees the torment on his face and sends him a message.

'Everyone here knows you are going to be the one that carries us through this. So please cheer up.'

Vargas was caught off guard by her kind words and flushes his doubts and fears out of his mind. He is a mage of lightning and apprenticed under one of the highest regarded sages alive Seleaf Mativ. He is good enough and he does deserve to be here.

2

They arrive at the Bastion Coliseum and drive up to the participant drop off at the front doors. There are physical flashing signs and digital advertisements everywhere, and the hum of conversation and flow of people feels almost the same as back in Pharis, just more frantic. Coach Hillborn tells everyone they have an hour before they have to register and to have a look around while he parks the bus.

The girls run off into the building and start to look for places to shop with Amber begin dragged behind them. Vargas takes him time and walks up the small staircase into the main lobby. It is one big circle with stores lined up all around the outside of the Coliseum with gambling machines in the inner circle. At the center of it all is the Coliseum floor and seating, which is where they are going to be participating.

As he walks around each digital advertisement pops up and is personalized to him with the data from his purchases from the digital wallet in his HaLO. He ignores most of them until one in particular catches his eye. It reads 'Would you like to know your fate, or perhaps just how you will do in the tournament? Find Fortune now!' He stops and looks at it with a surprised look because he hasn't yet registered for the tournament, so how did this advertisement know that.

"Well my friend that is the magic for Fortune." says a voice from behind Vargas with a strange accent. He quickly turns around to see a small caramel skinned man with teeth of silver.

"My name is Fortune, and I know you were participating in the tournament Vargas because that is what I do."

"Ok....weird, but what can you tell me and how much does it cost?"

"I will give it to you now, and you can pay me later, I know you will be good for it."

"Alright, so what can you tell me?"

"Sacrifice is not the only way to power, beware the lure."

"Is that it?"

"That is free advice for the day, and it may not sink into that adolescent head of yours until it is too late but I have given you your fortune. I will give you one other piece of advice, the other boy I came here to see today will be strong, keep an eye on him, because he will be an ally."

Vargas confused slightly tilts his head, "And who might that be?"

"That is for you to decide." Says Fortune with a shinning smile.

Bailey Jacobs, the team captain, looks over to Vargas and sees him standing in place, and as far as she can tell, talking to himself. "Vargas!" She yells at him

He turns and looks over at her, "What do you want?"

"What are you doing over there?"

"Can't you see I'm talking to..." Vargas turns his head back to where Fortune was, only to see that there is nothing there. The booth and small tent that was behind Fortune was all gone. But there is a message waiting to be read on his HaLO. It reads '*Advice when most needed, is least heeded*'. Bailey walks over to him and gives him a funny look. He finishes what he was going to say, "Well I was talking with someone and it looks like they aren't here any longer."

"You're not going all loopy on me are you Vargas. I need you to at least be able to swipe your HaLO over the check in reader. Think you can do that." She remarks sarcastically.

"Yea yea, I think I can handle that." he replies letting the comment go.

Registration had started and they walked over as a group and were first in line to get themselves set up as the Pharis Magitecks. Their placements were all set up and they all swiped their HaLO's over the registration scanner. The receptionist tells the group that they will all need to take all of their possessions and go to the rune scanner to register their belongings. Vargas walks through the scanner and has no problems getting through because he doesn't use runes.

Bailey, on the other hand, was the only one of the group that had trouble getting through the scanners. She is a technology specialist and uses tech to augment her spells. One of those was a rune pistol she uses for long range attacks. The two Paladins that were doing the scanning told her that she had to check it in and use what will be provided.

She questioned why, and they went on to explain that the officials today are going to be Paladins and the Captain Commander, Tyler Hemlic, is going to be presiding over the tournament today. This news made Vargas' ears perk up a bit. If the Commander of the Paladins is going to be here for this, they have to be looking for recruits.

This could be the chance that he was looking for when he joined this MMA team. The Paladins get a good salary, do good work that he could be proud of and he could get recognition for it. Perfect! Vargas starts running through everything in his head that he can do that will give him a shot to win and help secure him a position in their recruitment.

The tournament is about to begin and right before the ramp to get onto the main floor where the opening ceremonies are about to be held. There are a few tables filled with Knight quality level runes of all shapes and sizes as well as holders for them for every place they can be held.

There is also a table with rune pistols of all different types.

Vargas looks over at Bailey and can see the drool building in her mouth over everything that is in front of her. She frantically goes back and forth amongst the different options, finally settling on roughly the same version of pistol she had.

The stage is surrounded with students from all around the continent. Center stage is the Astrum government insignia, is an red arbor shape with a white shooting star traveling across it from the lower left toward the upper right surrounded within a circle filled in with stars. As Tyler walks onto the stage the crowd of high school students goes silent.

The coliseum seating filled to bursting and looks alive with the number of people that are pouring into their seats with the start nearing. The displays around the coliseum light up and focus on Tyler's face. The coliseum goes silent.

"People of Eden, I would like to extend my personal gratitude for your attendance today. My name is Tyler Hemlic, I am the Captain Commander of the Paladin Order and I will be your Master of Ceremonies here today. We all have been given a great honor here to witness the first official High School Mixed Magical Arts Tournament, and our gracious host The City of Bastion is to thank for these glorious and luscious facilities. Today we are here to witness the preliminary matches for the main tournament which is to be held in New Atlantis in one month's time, and the points system will be in effect today. There will also be extra points awarded to schools with a surprise addition of one on one matches, and a free for all match to end the tournament here today. The free for all, and one on one matches are voluntary but could give as much points overall for the winners as the main bout here today. Students will be receiving a HaLO prompt momentarily that will allow you to register for one or both of the extra challenges today.

"Extending out his left arm with his index and middle finger out, waves his fingers around in a circle, then swipes to the right. He begins to say a prayer over the students as their HaLOs activate with an overlay message. Three options appear in the middle of their vision;

None; One on One; Free for All.

Vargas without hesitation signs up for both and hits ok.

"That being settled, we can begin the setup for the one on one matches. We will have four separate tiers going at the same time on this floor. They will be separated off, and walls added in just for this round. Once completed, the top four will face off to determine the winner of the one on one matches. We will then continue onto the group matches, to conclude the tournament today we will have a free for all match. May

lady luck smile upon you all here in Bastion,
and let the tournament begin!"

3

The officials brought out onto the coliseum floor a shield generator to split the area into four roughly equal parts. They have also split the rankings so you didn't have to fight your teammates in the early rounds if they also opted in. During the registration, the form had a listing for your team mates, starting with the team captain.

Vargas got put into group 3 since he was third seat, and he sees that Bailey also opted into these rounds and she got put into group 1. Her group set up quicker than his, and he decides to look over at the match. As the match starts and ends in a split second.

A black haired boy had moved behind his opponent so fast that Vargas couldn't see it happen but what he did see was the massive cylinder of ice that was thrusted at the opponent and broke through the shield in between groups 1 and 2. He looks at the boy and their glances connect. He can see concern in the boys icy blue eyes and on his face.

Vargas has a smirk grow across his face and nods in an approving manner. The boys face relaxes and he can see the relief there. Vargas knows now that he will be the one to beat in this tournament and is called up to his first match.

Every other school had set up the teams in regards to strength not clout like what Pharis had done. This made things very easy on Vargas though. Blasting though each of his rounds with ease and he didn't even have to use anything Sel had taught him yet.

With the first round of the one on one matches complete it was now time for the real fights to begin. His fight was against the boy that he locked eyes with from group 1, Vernon Douglas. The official walks over in between and looks to the left and right at both boys, and asks if they are both ready. They both nod, and the official raises their right hands and then quickly brings them down shouting begin!

"You'd better be ready." Vernon boasts

Vargas remembered the way he opens and needs to be faster. He uses the first technique that his Master Sel had taught him. Focusing the flow of his magic within his body to align it over all of his nerves, charging them, and giving him a quicker reaction time. This had taken him a year just to use it.

"Try me!" Vargas yells

Wind gathers beneath Vernon's feet as he bursts forward, clearing the distance quickly. Vargas can see him this time and lays down a lightning wall spell onto the ground. He creates an arch of lightning at his feet and floats backwards across it, to avoid being hit by either Vernon or his spell.

21

Vernon passes over the spot he touched which creates a wall of lightning with him right in the middle. He passes through and gets covered in electricity, hitting the ground writhing in pain, and rolls to a stop. Vargas moves quickly by gliding over to where his opponent landed and thinks to himself he might be able to intimidate this guy off of his game plan. Standing over Vernon, looking down at him.

"You have quite a bit of speed, but you're not faster than I am, I can ride lightning. I saw how you beat your other opponents. You use your speed to close the distance, and your strength to overwhelm. Sadly, you won't be able to be so predictable against me Rune Master Vernon Douglas, you'll have to do better than that." Vargas finishes as he gathers magic into his hand forming bolts of lightning into two bluish purple spheres, as streaks shoot from his hands to the ground.

Vernon barely wind bursts away from the blast, sliding away from Vargas. Getting up he brushes himself off. Vargas sees him glancing down which must be to his overlay, and does the same. His readout shows his current mana reserves and luckily he has barely used any.

His opponent, on the other hand, doesn't seem to be deterred by his attempt at intimidation. Vernon slams down his palm to the ground releasing energy from his runes as ice flows out in all directions to cover over half the two hundred yard coliseum floor. Vargas' feet are caught within the thick ice, just over his toes and up over the back of his heel.

"Let's see how fast you are now!" Vernon shouts

Vargas replies with a smirk across his face, "Good play Rune Master but you failed to realize what I said earlier, I *ride* the lightning." He shows Vernon what he means as he shatters the layer of ice covering his shoes by the souls of his shoes shatter the layer of ice covering them.

He floats above the ice that Vernon just laid down atop arcs of lightning under his feet. Leaning forward the bolts reach out and take him across the frost covered floor.

Stopping abruptly in front of Vernon. Vernon flinches bringing his fists up to cover his face. Vargas takes this opportunity to use the second thing that Master Sel had taught him. He uses the extra magic around him to charge himself and his attacks similar to what an elemental mage does in a transformation.

Arcs of electricity start flowing out of Vargas' back as if he spread skeletal wings of lightning. He can see the look in Vernon's face as he stands there in awe.

This only last but for a moment, and then he smirks. "I heard you plain and clear, Lightning Mage Vargas." He says, making a closing gesture with his hands.

The ice beneath Vargas closes as two halves of a sphere come together around him. He can hear a muffled voice from the other side say, '*Hot la ow.*' He isn't quite sure if that was what he said, but that is what he heard.

The inside would have been dark if not for the wings at his back. He needs to get out and fast, but getting out will take a large amount of strain. Trying to lessen it he looks down and can see the dirt on the ground. Pulling in mana from the ground beneath him, he folds it into a lightning bolt, releasing it toward the sky.

The ice shell bursts open with a frantic rage of sparks and shards of ice flying everywhere. The bolt of lightning heads toward the top of the coliseum and hits the shield guarding the crowd with a great thunder of sizzles and pops.

Standing there radiating heat off his shoulders, wings spread and pulsing, gather up for an attack. The shield above flickers and sputters to get back to full power. Vargas locates Vernon. He must have been knocked back from the blast and released a pillar of ice behind him he had planed on attacking him with.

Vargas sees he is still off balance and makes a move before he gets the chance to block. Forming a blade of plasma he swings at Vernon, connecting with his left shoulder. The weight of the swing takes him to his knees, as the air cracks and pops.

Following up to make sure he stays down he sends a bolt through the ground which connects effortlessly with the underside of Vernon's chin sending him flying in the air a few feet off the ground. He comes crashing down on his back with a thud, and cloud of dust. Finally hoping to finish the match Vargas launches a volley of quick lightning strikes as quickly as he can.

Vargas waits for the dust to clear before noticing that his stasis shield has not activated yet. He walks over to where Vernon is laying, and sees he is just laying there with his eyes closed. He can see he's in pain and was hit by everything and can't seem to figure why the match hasn't been concluded yet.

Vargas says with sympathy is his voice, "You do know how to take a hit Rune Master."

"Just end it without too much gloating if you don't mind." Vernon replies quickly.

"As you wish, I will make it quick." Vargas replies.

Reaching up with his right hand into the air, clouds appear and turn black. A rumble of thunder rolls throughout the coliseum as the thunderstorm grows in strength. The air smells like a brewing storm as the first lightning bolt strikes his right hand.

Vargas feels the pressure from the strike, and the proceeding four, almost take him to his knees. The lightning travels through his body to his left hand, forming a white ball of pulsing energy. Now pointing at Vernon he braces himself for one last bolt.

The sky flashes, and seats rumble as all the newly formed clouds in the coliseum light up at once, discharging into Vargas' hand. It all comes out at Vernon, his body jumping a few feet in the air as the cloud fade away to the clear sky up above.

The crowd collectively gasps as his body falls back to the ground. Steam coming off his shoulders his wings dissipate and he starts breathing heavily from the over use and combination of techniques. He had used the third technique taught to him. Passing an element through your body and charging it with your mana to create an exponential effect. But what he didn't know was the toll it took when used at full strength.

Looking to Vernon, the impact left him there life less, but still no stasis shell. Vargas walks over to the judge and asks, "Judge, can we call the match here, the poor guy is out cold and I don't want to hit him again just to try to get the stasis shield to work?"

"Let me check him." The Judge kneels down to Vernon and checks his pulse, and can't feel anything. He grabs his HaLO to pull data off of it. He receives an error message

"Commander, I have a HaLO I can't access the data for, can I call the match?

He is knocked out but not in stasis?"
Vargas overhears the Judge muttering into
his HaLO.

"Ignore it, and continue? Are you sure
sir, the kid is pretty beat up... Understood...,
yes sir..., sorry sir." The Judge turns
around, and looks at Vargas, "The match
can't be called till you stasis him. We have
determined that the contestants stasis
device is functioning properly and within
expected levels. You can resume the
match."

Vargas stands there for a second, not
knowing what to do. He looks down at
Vernon, who he doesn't even see breathing,
and he has to keep attack him to win?
Vargas wants to win, but not over some
ones safety like this. He starts to think about
giving up, when Vernon gasps for air.

He slowly starts to get up, first to his
knees and then stumbles to his feet.
Vargas is baffled by what he is looking at,
this guy was next to dead from what it
seemed, to now be standing, is daunting.
He is relieved that he isn't dead or severely
injured since this is only supposed to be
competition not some sort of death match.

"How are you doing Vernon?" Vargas
asks with concern in his voice

"That was a good hit but I guess it
wasn't enough to finish the match." Vernon
yells and immediately drops to one knee.
He raises his head slowly.

"Are you sure you are alright?"

"I'll be fine, and thanks."

"The Judge says that we have to continue till we get stasis'd, so are you good enough to continue?"

"I think so." Vernon stands, "I might have just gotten my second wind."

"Ha ha ha..., well that is good to hear. Let us continue then."

Vargas walks back to the starting point and Vernon follows. Vernon digs his right foot into the ground and makes a dash toward Vargas. He is moving faster than he started out with and he didn't use his rune to increase his speed.

The first punch comes in fast and he's barely able to dodge it as Vernon's fist grazes his cheek. Vargas quickly refocuses on his first technique, to quicken his movements, just in time to block with both forearms a left roundhouse kick. The impact almost knocks him to the ground. In that instance he catches a glimpse of Vernon's eyes which have turned completely black.

Each punch comes in faster and faster, and he has to start using more and more magic just to block and avoid getting hit. He can feel the strain on his body worsening and he knows he won't last long once Vernon starts connecting.

Every dodge brushing clothes or skin, while each hit rattles his bones. He can feel himself wearing down, almost about to give out. His will to win is the only thing keeping him up.

He jumps back putting the butt of his palms together forcing what magic he has left to gather as sparks fly from the tips of his fingers to his palms. It creates a ball of plasma which discharges at Vernon with a fearsome thunderous blast. It travels quickly but Vernon still had time to react and brace for impact.

It lands square in his hands, pushing him back, feet dragging across the ground. Vernon grips the ball shattering it as if was made of glass and it dissipates like dust in the wind.

Vargas vision is blurring slightly but he still can't believe what he just saw. Vernon's hands and forearms are glowing black. He believed he was just rune user, but he clearly has access to some type of magic to shatter his spell like that. He has also never seen a spell dissipate before but doesn't have time now to contemplate it.

With not much left on his side, he draws from the magic around him for a larger attack. Plasma begins to form in the palms of each of his hands, each larger than his last attack.

Vernon again rushes Vargas to close in. Vargas grabs down on the plasma balls, turning them into blades. Swinging them both in horizontally, Vernon stops both blades with his hands unfazed. Gripping down on them and they shatter like glass, and before Vargas can blink, Vernon's fist is planted into his stomach.

The punch itself vibrates throughout his whole body. A pillar of black light pierces through before it retracts back to Vernon's fist.

The mana he has left inside of him feels like it is boiling him alive and ready to explode but all he can do is lurch forward expelling what breath he has. The boiling begins to fade slightly before the second punch comes across his chin, and a spinning cone of black light comes out of the other side of his face.

This spins him around as he drops to the ground, and Vernon now stands above looking down. Vargas notices this time a draining feeling that came with the light. As if his connection to magic was being cut off.

Vernon's eyes slowly regain their blue color again, as he stumbles backward. His heel catching a small break in the ground from the fight and falls to the ground. Vargas still on the ground himself struggles to find the strength to stand, amazed by what just transpired. First getting to his knee, followed by standing, with a great amount of effort to stay that way.

He tries to gather magic and is unable to call it forth. He closes his eyes for a second and to refocus his efforts on what Sel had taught him by gathering the magic from around him, to only get a spark. Opening his eyes he sees Vernon still on the ground and in an instant, the stasis shell covers him.

Letting out a sigh of accomplishment, a smile come over his face only for a second. Why did his stasis shell just activate. He was in the losing ground right there at the end and then he went down.

The Paladin watching the bout walks over and declares Vargas the winner of that match, and the crowd stayed silent for a moment not sure about what just happened but eventually erupted into cheers. His next bout was against Duke Keragus from the same school as Vernon but was in group 2.

This match went quickly. Vargas was still overly exhausted from the last match. His flow of magic returned but he was too physically spent without having Amber or another healer treat him to use his techniques. Vargas decides to settle for second place.

4

Once he got back into the locker room Bailey was first to tell him how well he did offering her congratulations on the second place spot and the extra points for their school. Amber looked over his body and told him that she didn't see any surface wounds other than some bruises. He leaned in and whispered to her that it was nerve and deep tissue damage and if she can treat that.

Looking alarmed she asks what happened. He just replies it was some techniques that he used that do that to him. She gave him an overly worried look, like a sister would, but begins to work her healing magic without pressing the subject. A bright white light covers his body and begins to accelerate his bodies own healing process.

She finishes healing him in time to be called back out to the floor for the team matches. The floor had changed to a tree filled environment with lush greenery, sweet fragrances and a breath of hot air as they walked in.

They surprisingly had a well balanced team, which was a happy surprise to Vargas. Shannon was in the front and kept her shield spells active or on the ready, Julie was able to distract the other team or conceal the group with her specialty in illusions. Bailey and himself were attackers, with Amber healing and mending the group as needed. The team challenges went by very quickly and without much incident. Most of the teams were so disorganized they couldn't coordinate with one another. They almost did as much harm to themselves as trying to attack Vargas' team.

The locker room had a powerful positive vibe going on between everyone. For the first time Vargas had truly felt he was a part of something that was more than himself and that he belonged. It was a feeling that he truly enjoyed.

Vargas looks at everyone and asks, "Did anyone sign up for the free for all coming up here in a second?"

"Yea, we all did." Bailey answers, "I asked everyone after I got knocked out of the one on one's but you were still out there winning."

"Awesome, so any plans?"

"Not really, no"

"Why do you got one?" Shannon says with a little skepticism.

"I think I just might. I know this trick that I learned recently, and it is only supposed to be for emergency situations but I want to see what it does. If you can keep a shield up and Julie conceal us long enough for me to prepare it I might just be able to get everyone in one go."

"You're crazy, you can't know something like that!" Julie says in disbelief.

"I learned it from Seleaf Mativ, the sage. I have been his apprentice of sorts for a few years now."

"Well that explains how you beat that guy earlier with those crazy skeletal lightning wings. For a second I thought you were an elemental and just hadn't been telling us."

"No I don't think I am, but I just really like and have an affinity toward it. When I am ready, I will tell you all to back away and move me out of the shield. I think it's going to be a big blast."

Every single student in the tournament signed up for the free for all, and they are all standing next to their other teammates. Vargas asks the girls if they are all ready, and they nod their heads.

Scanning the crowd he can see that most of the people there are staring at Vernon's group. He thought for sure that since they had won all of their team matches they would be targeted first but they had somehow managed to fly under the radar.

With the official's go, the coliseum floor turns into a magical war zone. Spells of all colors, sizes, and elements are flying every which way. The once lush greenery gets repeatedly pummeled from the barrage. Frozen and shattered, burnt to a crisp, the earth beneath it split in twain and the smells of all mix in the air.

Vargas starts drawing the rune in the dirt and stands in the center of it. He closes his eyes and imagines the rune drawing on the ground filling up with his power. It slowly gains a viridian glow and Vargas' head starts to feel woozy but remains concentrated. Master Sel had told him that something like that might happen.

With the rune filled it starts to softly vibrate and give off a soothing hum of energy. He looks back at the girls and gives them the signal to step backwards. He goes through each of the techniques shown to him before activating the rune. He aligns his flow of magic over his body and nerves once more, followed by drawing in magic from around him to let his wings of lightning form. They spread open wide, and fully plumed out like wings on a bird from all the extra magic.

As he emerges from the retreating shield and invisibility spell, the battle stops. Everyone turns and stares at him floating above a viridian glowing rune. The hair on every ones head begins to discharge static and stand on end. The smell of the air ionizes. The coliseum is quiet save for the hum of electricity coming from Vargas.

His hands and arms are encroached with electricity. Opening them wide he activates the rune, and turns himself into a conduit for his lightning. He releases thousands of bolts of lightning within the blink of an eye.

The displays show nothing but white and the whole crowd stands and rushes the edge to try to see what is going on. Vargas' father leans back into his seat with a smile on his face. As the rune fades it burns a crater into the ground and Vargas collapses into it as it blackens.

The lightning fades from him followed by everyone else. He slowly tries to stand and glances around to see that only a few participants that are not stasised before he collapses and falls face first to the ground, and into stasis himself.

He wakes to Seleaf's face smiling over him on one side and his father's smile on the other. Amber, Julie, Shannon, and Bailey are all in the room as well but are at the end of the recovery table. Taking in a deep breath he feels extraordinary, knowing he should be sore.

"So you used the rune I showed you....when it wasn't an emergency." Sel says with a small amount of aggravation in his voice.

"Sorry Master Sel, I just wanted to see it work and wanted to win this."

"Son you were amazing, but you shouldn't risk your own life like that."

"What do you mean?"

"Like I told you, the rune is emergency only and you made it way too big. It uses your life force to overcharge your spells. If you use too much, you die, and you almost did. Luckily I was here to see another pupil of mine and saw you use it. I come down here to aid you." says Sel

"Thanks Master, you are a lifesaver."

"Alright everyone go back to the locker room and gather your things, your teacher will be here shortly." Sel says, and everyone starts to grab their things and head out of the locker room.

"Son, I'll head out and get the car. Like I said the other day I am going to take you home myself. I already talked to Coach Hillborn and he said it was ok."

"Alright dad, see you in a minute." Vargas says as he gets up and off the table.

"Now that everyone is gone let me tell you what I did for you." Sel says in a commanding tone

"I had to use a special magic to replenish your life force. It's called cypher energy and you can only get it one way and is very *difficult* to get."

"Wow, I have never heard of anything like that before."

"There are maybe ten people in the world that I know of that can extract it, let alone use it."

"Incredible, is that why I feel so amazing right now?"

"Yes, it is. Since you know this now, you cannot share that information with anyone and there are things I am going to need to teach you. You are going to become a true apprentice of mine and I will start showing you how to fully use what I have already shown you."

"You have done so much for me and showed me so many things already, it would be an honor to be your apprentice." Vargas says with excitement of learning more.

Sel says with excitement in his voice, "Excellent, because there are many things left to learn, many many things."

Mark Brandon Powell

Other Stories By the Author

Cypher Theorem: The Zero Class

More Coming Soon!

About the Author

Mark Brandon Powell, creator of the Cypher Theorem series, born and raised in Texas. He writes because he wants tell epic stories, and journeys.

Visit

www.MarkBrandonPowell.com